Susan Meddaugh

MARTHA CALLING

sandpiper

HOUGHTON MIFFLIN HARCOURT
BOSTON • NEW YORK

For Niko, Harry, Sandy, and *Poppa*

www.houghtonmifflinbooks.com

Library of Congress Cataloging-in-Publication Data

Meddaugh, Susan.
    Martha calling / Susan Meddaugh
    p. cm.
    Summary: When she wins a call-in radio contest, Martha the talking dog and her family go for a vacation and manage to change the "no dogs allowed" policy.
    RNF ISBN-13: 978-0-395-69825-9
    PA ISBN-13: 978-0-395-82741-3
    [1. Dogs—Fiction. 2. Vacations—Fiction.] I. Title.
    PZ7.M51273Mao   1994   93-50611
    [E]—dc20   CIP
                                 AC

Manufactured in Singapore
TWP 20 19 18 17 16 15 14 13 12

Martha was always a talented dog.

But when she ate alphabet soup, something truly surprising happened. The letters went up to her brain instead of down to her stomach . . .

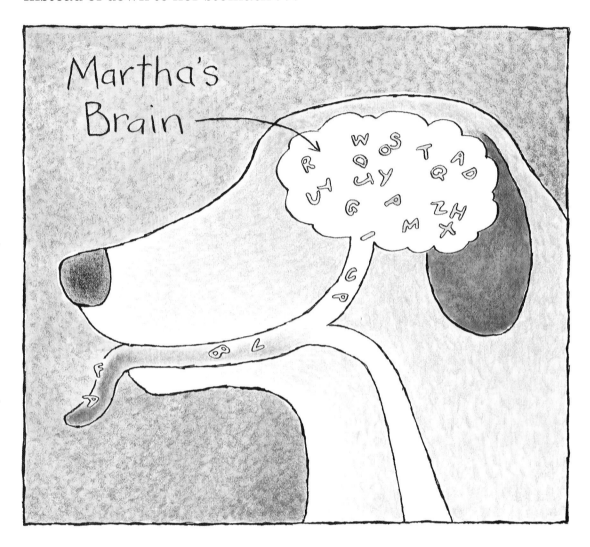

and Martha spoke.

Martha loved letters. She lapped up consonants, and savored every tender vowel.
Martha loved words. Lots of them. Separately, or strung together in endless sentences.

But there were three words Martha hated.

These words meant she was never welcome in restaurants . . .

or in any of her favorite stores.

And people were so rude.

This was confusing to Martha because when she called the same places on the telephone, people were always polite. On the telephone they never said: "Hey! Are you a dog? I'm hanging up if you're a dog!"

Martha loved the telephone. She could talk for hours.

One day she entered a contest.

Martha won a free weekend for four at the cozy Come-On-Inn.
Her family was thrilled.
But when the official notice came in the mail,
there was a problem.

"I have an idea," said Helen. She and Martha disappeared into the attic. When they emerged:

Martha's family packed plenty of alphabet soup and set off for a wonderful weekend at the Come-On-Inn.

A small crowd had gathered to welcome them, and Helen introduced her grandma, *Martha*.
"Congratulations, Martha!" said the manager of the inn. "These flowers are for you."

But Martha was not interested in flowers.

Martha's family rushed her past the other guests
and up the hill to their room.

"Let's go for a swim," said Father.
"Then we can have a game of Ping-Pong," said Helen.
"And a nice picnic lunch," added Mother.
"Sounds like fun," said Martha.
But Mother said, "Sorry, Martha."
"I'll sneak you out after dark," said Helen.

"Sit and stay," said Father.
"Hmmmph!" thought Martha. "Same old story."

Confined to the room, Martha was depressed . . . until her eyes fell upon an old friend.

Her belly full, Martha fell into a deep sleep.
She didn't hear a soft knock on the door. She didn't wake up
when the chambermaid came in to leave fresh towels.
Then the chambermaid saw the bones,

the empty wheelchair,

and Martha.

She ran screaming from the room.

That woke Martha up. She wandered down the hall
to find out what was going on.

"Of course I'm mad," Martha said.
Everyone stopped and stared in absolute disbelief.

I won this contest, fair and square.
Me. Martha. And I'm not having any
fun at all. Why? Because I'm
a dog. D. O. G. Dog. A smart dog.
But... there are NO DOGS ALLOWED
in this hotel. Everywhere I go —
No Dogs Allowed! The Butcher
Shop... the Supermarket... No
Dogs Allowed!
I CAN'T BELIEVE
IT! Dogs have
been by your side
since you were
in caves. Ten
thousand years of
loyalty, and we
still can't go into
a restaurant and
order a steak.

"Why is everybody leaving?" asked Mother when the family returned from their swim.
"Uh-oh," said Helen. She spotted Martha . . . sitting with the manager.

But the manager was smiling.
"I wonder if Grandma, I mean Martha, would be interested in summer employment?"

The next day, the cozy Come-On-Inn got a new name, and Martha started her summer job. Pets are now welcome at the Sit-n-Stay Hotel, where the soup du jour is always alphabet, and the hostess is never at a loss for words. Business is grrreat!